The Most Awesome Dream Ever

Isaiah Valera

ELEVATION
CONSULTING

D1517786

Library of Congress Cataloging-in-Publication Data
(Pending)
ISBN: 9798558357363
Printed in the United States of America

Elevation Consulting LLC | Book company
ElevationConsultingGlobal.com
Book Cover & Ilustrations by: Wilmer Fiore

CONTENTS

CHAPTER 1

How the kid had the dream

Tim ate dinner and then got his iPad. It's nighttime and Tim is watching YouTube videos about the moon, because he hopes one day to travel to the moon with his dad. Then he hears his dad's voice say, *"Tim it's time for bed."* And Tim responds, *"Oh, really?"* *"Yes!"* said Lee. Tim goes to bed. His dad reminds him, *"Make sure you sleep well because tomorrow you have a test."* Tim went to sleep and had the coolest dream ever. His dream was that he went with his dad to the moon and build the biggest moon base.

Keep dreaming!

CHAPTER 2

The moon

Tim and Lee went to the moon and they were very excited, because they were going to build a moon base. But first they looked around the moon. One spot had a lot of aliens. The aliens were finding things for their Sci-fi boss. He was very bossy! He told all the aliens to do stuff for him and for the moon, but he didn't care about the moon. Lee and Tim said hi to an alien. The alien responded, *"WE ARE BUSY!"* And then Lee and Tim said hi to another alien, the alien also said, *"WE ARE BUSY!"* Tim replied, "Ok." Tim and Lee started to write the idea for the moon base. They got a notebook. An alien said, *"NOTEBOOKS ARE NOT ALLOWED IN THE MOON!"* Tim replied, *"We are just writing the idea for the moon base."* The alien went to tell the Sci-fi boss. The Sci-fi boss said to the alien, *"If they break one more rule you bring them to me."*

Go as high as the moon

CHAPTER 3

Building the moon base

Tim and Lee were done writing their idea for the moon. They started building the moon base. First, they built the first floor. Next, they built the second floor. And third, they built the third floor. Then they made up a name for the moon base it was called, The Most Awesome Moon Base. Then they went inside and had a party. Aliens went to the party too. They all started to play music. Sci-fi boss was not happy because he needed the aliens to do stuff. So, he went to the moon base. And told Tim and Lee to stop the party. The sci-fi boss angrily said, "*I need the aliens to do work.*" Tim and Lee said, "*No.*" Sci-fi boss said then I am going to talk with you two.

Be creative and start building!

CHAPTER 4

The talk with the sci-fi boss, the king of the moon

The aliens took Tim and Lee to the Sci-fi boss moon base. They had a talk. First, Sci-fi boss said, *"You know I am the boss of the moon."* Tim and Lee were scared because He was the boss of the moon and thought, *"Maybe he will harm us!"* Tim and Lee said, *"Well you are bossy."* Sci-fi boss said to Lee and Tim, *"Oh my gosh."* *"I am sorry,"* Tim and Lee said. *"Me to,"* said Sci-fi boss. They all realized they were best friends from a long time ago.

Express yourself by talking

CHAPTER 5

Saving the people

They wanted to be nice and kind, so they went looking for people that were in the moon for years. First, they went to the very back of the moon. They saw 20 people, they tooked them to the moon base. Next, they went to the right side of the moon. They also saw 20 people. Then, they went to the left side of the moon. They also saw 20 people. Last, they went to the front of the moon. They saw 10 people.

Always help people

CHAPTER 6

The new house

When they were done saving the people, they saw a new house. It was very big. They went inside. There were three floors. They were amazed. They really wanted the house but there was an owner. They needed to pay $10,000 to get it. They only had $1,000, and they gave all the money to the owner. The owner said, *"Great job! You can have this house for the rest of your life."* But the owner said one more thing, *"If you break one thing in this house, you are not getting it and you will go back to planet earth even if you are an alien."*

Be thankful for your home

CHAPTER 7

They got furniture

The new house was empty. So, they had to get furniture. First, they went to the back of the moon. They saw 30 things for the house. Next, they went to the right of the moon, they saw 20 things. Then, they went to the left of the moon, they saw 10 things for the house. Last, they went to the front of the moon, they saw 40 things for the house. And then they put everything in the new house.

Furniture makes a house feel like a home

CHAPTER 8

The scientist

When they were done putting the things in the house, they saw a scientist. The scientist name was Freddy. The scientist said, *"Do you want me to do experiments for you?"* Then everyone said, *"Yes!"* Then the scientist did the experiment. The scientist was so good that everyone allowed him to stay in the house. But the scientist was a bad guy and he stole things from everyone, and he stole one thing from the house. An alien caught him stealing that one thing. The scientist said sorry to everyone and he put the thing back.

Never take what is not yours

CHAPTER 9

They both live together

The scientist was so ashamed. Everyone saw that he was very sad, so they said, *"You can live in this house."* The scientist said, *"Thank you but I need to bring all of my stuff to this house."* He also said, *"My house is one mile away so it's not that far."* Everyone said, *"We will help you."* So, they all bought the stuff back and made a room for the scientist.

Be happy with the people you live with!

CHAPTER 10

The end

Tim woke up. He said, *"WOW what a dream!"* He went downstairs. He did not see anyone. Not Mom Not Lee not anyone. And then He said ***THE MOON BASE BOOK TWO HAS JUST BEGUN!***

The book is finished, but life's adventure never ends!

About the author

Isaiah Valera is a creative and fun-loving eight-year-old. He enjoys singing, dancing and all forms of arts. This is Isaiah's first book and he's already working on his second book. His parents are from the Dominican Republic, but he was born and lives in New Jersey.

Made in the USA
Middletown, DE
13 November 2020

23950051R00027